Moosejaw
Means
Business

THE GOOSE PIMPLE BAY · SAGAS ·

Ma Moosejaw Means Business

Karen Wallace
Illustrated by Nigel Baines

A & C Black · London

For Katie J, with thanks

First published 2007 by
A & C Black Publishers Ltd
38 Soho Square, London, W1D 3HB

www.acblack.com

Text copyright © 2007 Karen Wallace
Illustrations copyright © 2007 Nigel Baines

The rights of Karen Wallace and Nigel Baines to be identified as
the author and illustrator of this work have been asserted by them in
accordance with the Copyrights, Designs and Patents Act 1988.

ISBN 978-0-7136-7973-1

A CIP catalogue for this book is available from the British Library.

This book is produced using paper that is made from wood
grown in managed, sustainable forests. It is natural, renewable and
recyclable. The logging and manufacturing processes conform
to the environmental regulations of the country of origin.

Printed and bound in Great Britain by MPG Books Limited.

Chapter One

Ma Moosejaw scratched her long, lumpy nose and looked down at the stone cottages along the shore of Goose Pimple Bay. "I mean business this time," she said to her husband, Chief Thunderstruck.

"What business?" Chief Thunderstruck had been thinking about food. It was a long walk up to the top of the cliff above the bay. Now he was hungry.

"We'll eat first," said Ma Moosejaw, taking a picnic from her bag. "There's flat bread with reindeer nuggets and honey cakes and berries."

Reindeer nuggets! Reindeer nuggets were Chief Thunderstruck's favourite. Ma Moosejaw must have some very important business on her mind.

"As you know, Thunderstruck," said Ma Moosejaw. "Our village was founded by my father, one of the greatest of us Vikings. When I married you, we took it over." She pointed down to a long, wooden building with a pointed roof. It was the Great Hall of Goose Pimple Bay and it was their home. "Now the time has come to pass it on to one of our sons."

"Why on earth would we want to do that?" Chief Thunderstruck choked on a piece of flat bread. "Both our sons are useless. Whiff Erik is a weedy wet, who stinks worse than a billy goat and Spike Carbuncle is plain mean and nasty."

"I know that," replied Ma Moosejaw, as she swallowed a reindeer nugget in one. "That's why they have to find themselves brides."

"Brides? No one would marry either of them," said Chief Thunderstruck.

"Well, they'll have to sort that out on their own," said Ma Moosejaw. "I'm not taking care of them any more." She stared at her husband. "Think about it, Thunderstruck, your beard is grey and, uh, I'm not as young as I used to be."

"That's true," said Chief Thunderstruck. Then he saw the look on his wife's face. "I mean about the colour of my beard, of course."

But now Ma Moosejaw wasn't listening. She had a wandering look in her eyes. "I want to see a white bear before I get too old," she said, suddenly.

"But those bears live in the far north," said Chief Thunderstruck. "We would have to go on a very long expedition."

"Exactly," said Ma Moosejaw. "My plan is for us to retire and go on holiday."

Chief Thunderstruck looked down at Goose Pimple Bay. The idea of getting away had never occurred to him before, but the more he thought about it, the more he liked it. "That's a brilliant plan!" he cried.

Ma Moosejaw stuffed the rest of the picnic back in the bag. "We'll eat the honey cakes on our way down," she said. "Let's talk to Whiff and Spike right away."

✳✳✳

It was already suppertime when Chief Thunderstruck and Ma Moosejaw opened the doors of the Great Hall.

A long table stretched from one end to the other. Both sides were packed with the men and women of Goose Pimple Bay and they were all eating and laughing.

Behind them, the walls were decorated with antlers, bearskins and leather shields. In between the shields, Whiff Erik had hung up bunches of dried herbs and flowers because he was a keen gardener. And in between the flowers, there was the glint of knife handles because Spike Carbuncle liked throwing daggers at the wall.

As Chief Thunderstruck and Ma Moosejaw stood by the door, they saw Spike Carbuncle leaning back on his chair and bragging to his friends about how he had trapped a bear single-handed.

Around him, the other Vikings were pretending to be impressed, even though everyone knew that Spike Carbuncle was afraid of the forest and never went there on his own – it was too dark and, when the wind blew, the branches made a scratchy noise that terrified him.

As for Whiff Erik, he was mixing his food into a mush, then making it look like a pie. And even over the smoke, the smell that hung around him filled the room.

Chief Thunderstruck could barely look at his sons. They were both such a waste of space.

Suddenly, for no reason, Spike Carbuncle banged down his mug on his wooden plate and pushed his nose into his brother's face.

"Sissy!" he sneered. "No real Viking brings back seeds and reptiles from his expeditions. He brings back gold and other people's jewellery, like me!" Spike spat a mouthful of beer into his brother's face. "I can smash a cottage door, steal everything valuable and set fire to the whole lot in less than five minutes!"

Whiff Erik ignored the beer dripping down his neck and bent down to feed his fire-breathing lizard a handful of red-hot chilies. He had found the lizard lying under a bush on his last winter expedition and noticed that every time it took a breath, more snow had melted around it. Now the lizard provided precious heat in the Great Hall.

"What good is gold and other's people jewellery when our father's feet are chilly and our mother's great nostrils are quivering with cold?" asked Whiff Erik. He pushed the lizard towards his mother and father as they took their places at the end of the table. "And what good is burning down other people's cottages when I bring back wonderful vegetables for us to eat?"

"Call this food?" Spike Carbuncle spat out his mouthful of green leaves. "I'd rather eat burnt bear meat!" Then his face took on a particularly nasty look. "And, by the way, you know that field behind the Great Hall," he said in a mean voice. "I'm putting a bear pit there!"

Whiff Erik felt anger surge through him. "That field's going to be my vegetable garden," he shouted.

"Oh, no, it isn't!" yelled Spike Carbuncle.

"Oh, yes, it is!"

"No!"

"Yes!"

"SILENCE!" Ma Moosejaw stood up and the Great Hall went quiet. "Your father and I have come to a decision."

She fixed Spike Carbuncle and Whiff Erik with blazing eyes. "You will both take your boats and leave at dawn to look for a bride."

"A *bride*?" squawked Whiff Erik and Spike Carbuncle, together. "Why?"

"Because I am sick of looking after you," replied Ma Moosejaw. "And you're both so useless, you can't look after yourselves."

"But—" It was the sound of two pathetic gulps.

"No buts," yelled Ma Moosejaw. "You will return with your brides by the next full moon." She lifted her great hand and banged it down on the table. "Whoever brings back the bride I like best will rule Goose Pimple Bay! The other will be banished to the forest for ever!"

The Hall was so quiet, everyone heard the fire-breathing lizard clear its throat.

What was going on?

"We are retiring," Chief Thunderstruck explained to the rows of puzzled faces. "And then we are going on holiday for a very, very long time."

Chapter Two

Two longboats with carved heads floated on the cold, grey waters in the harbour of Goose Pimple Bay. One was called the *Stealthy Stoat* and belonged to Spike Carbuncle. But even though its head was carved out of wood, there was nothing wooden about the *Stealthy Stoat*. It was as mean and nasty as its captain.

The other boat was called the *Dithering Duck* and it belonged to Whiff Erik. Although he had to admit that the *Dithering Duck* often talked rubbish – "life is not a pot of seaweed," it once quacked, and "what goes around often bounces" –

Whiff Erik never questioned its decisions at sea. The *Dithering Duck* was a bird, after all, and they always managed to arrive at the right place.

Just like the two brothers, the two boats hated each other.

"You haven't got a chance, you feather-brained nitwit," snarled the *Stealthy Stoat*. "Spike Carbuncle will bring home the best bride and Ma Moosejaw will banish Whiff Erik to the forest for ever."

"May the best boat bring back the best bride," said the *Dithering Duck*. "And don't forget, stoats can't swim."

"I don't need to swim," snapped the stoat. "I have a brain."

"Stoats stink," replied the *Dithering Duck*.

"Ducks are dumb," muttered the *Stealthy Stoat*.

And on they bickered until the stars disappeared and the sun rose.

✳✳✳

"See you later, sucker," yelled Spike Carbuncle as he jumped on board the *Stealthy Stoat* with his friend Axehead. "I'll be back with the best bride before you've even left!"

But Whiff Erik and his friend Slime Fungus were too busy putting away supplies to reply. As Whiff Erik wrapped his recipe book in reindeer skin to keep it dry, a lovely picture floated into his mind. It was from a dream he'd had the night before. Whiff Erik almost hugged himself for joy. He'd dreamt about a pretty girl with blonde hair and blue eyes. And he was sure she was going to be his bride!

Suddenly a clump of slimy seaweed landed on his head. Spike Carbuncle howled with laughter as the *Stealthy Stoat* sped past and headed out to sea.

"Things will look better in the morning," said the *Dithering Duck* kindly.

"It *is* the morning," replied Whiff Erik, pulling the seaweed out of his hair.

"Uh, OK," muttered the *Dithering Duck*. "How about the night time is the right time?"

"How about you set us a course and we get going?" said Whiff Erik, patiently.

"A duck knows his duty," squawked the *Dithering Duck* and soon Goose Pimple Bay was no more than a smudge on the horizon.

✳✳✳

Two days later, a great black cloud appeared, the wind grew stronger and the waves got bigger.

"What's happening?" asked Axehead, who was sitting sharpening his knife.

Spike Carbuncle felt a drop of rain fall on his face. "Dunno. Maybe we're near land." He turned to the *Stealthy Stoat*. "Any suggestions, Stoat?"

The *Stealthy Stoat* was so terrified he could barely speak. He had never been in a proper storm before and this one  looked like it was going to be really fierce.

"Bad weather," said the *Stealthy Stoat* in a choked voice. "Lost. Need a compass."

"What's a compass?" asked Axehead.

"Round thing with nails sticking out of it. The bit of string tells us where we're going," explained Spike.

"Oh, that," said Axehead. "It stuck into me when I sat on it so I threw it overboard."

The *Stealthy Stoat* thought he was going to be sick. Without a compass, he had no idea where he was or what to head for. There was only one thing to do. He had to find the *Dithering Duck*. He scanned the seas and as they rose on a huge wave, he caught sight of a tiny sail.

"Follow the duck!" cried the *Stealthy Stoat*. "That dumb Erik will never look over his shoulder, so he won't know we're behind him!"

Spike Carbuncle laughed. "Smart thinking, Stoat," he replied.

✳✳✳

The *Dithering Duck* was used to storms. He liked the feel of the wind in his feathers. There was only one problem. He couldn't make up his mind which way to go because he didn't have a compass.

mmmm...
...eermm..

"But you're a bird," protested Whiff Erik, as Slime Fungus tied down the supplies so they didn't get washed overboard. "You're supposed to have a compass in your head."

The *Dithering Duck* looked puzzled and shook his head just to make sure there wasn't a compass inside.

Nothing rattled.

"I must have forgotten to put it in," he said, sadly.

Whiff Erik threw up his hands in despair. "You're supposed to *know* where we should go!" he shouted.

"Oh," said the duck. "Nobody told me that." He tilted his head again and thought hard. Then suddenly he knew exactly what to do. He was a duck, after all!

Chapter Three

It was a black night with no moon when the *Dithering Duck* finally sailed into a rocky cove. But, just as the *Stealthy Stoat* had guessed, Whiff Erik never thought to look over his shoulder so he had no idea that Spike Carbuncle was right behind him.

High up on the cliff, a row of cottages glinted in the moonlight. It was quiet and peaceful, as the people who lived inside were sound asleep.

"What do you suggest, stealthiest of creatures?" whispered Spike Carbuncle as the *Stealthy Stoat* slid up the shore, as far away from the *Dithering Duck* as possible.

"Grab everything they've got and go home," replied the *Stealthy Stoat* without a second thought.

Spike Carbuncle chewed his lips. "What about my, uh—?"

"Bride?"

"Yeah. How do I, uh—?"

"Steal one," replied the *Stealthy Stoat* firmly. "Put her in a sack and stuff her below deck."

Spike Carbuncle flashed a black-toothed smile. "Thanks, Stoat!" Then he jumped overboard and waded to the shore.

❊❊❊

Things on board the *Dithering Duck* were a bit different. No one had a plan.

"What do you advise, finest of featherbrains?" asked Whiff Erik.

"It's a bit dark," said the duck, anxiously. "You can't see much in the dark."

"But there's a row of cottages up there," said Whiff Erik, looking at the cliff. "That means there are people here."

"We'll be able to see them more clearly in the daytime," replied the duck. "Things will look better in the morning," he added, helpfully.

Whiff Erik sighed. Perhaps the *Dithering Duck* was right. Everyone was tired and there was no sign of the *Stealthy Stoat* and Spike Carbuncle so at least there wouldn't be any trouble. He patted the duck's neck. "Thanks, Duck."

Then Whiff Erik rolled himself up in a sail and went to sleep beside Slime Fungus. And all night long he dreamed of a pretty girl with blonde hair and blue eyes.

✳✳✳

As soon as Whiff Erik woke up and saw the row of cottages on fire, he knew that Spike Carbuncle must have landed there as well.

"What am I going to do now?" he asked Slime Fungus. "Everyone will think we're like Spike because we're Vikings, too."

Slime Fungus nodded glumly.

"But what about my bride?" wailed Whiff Erik. "After this, no one will talk to us and I'll never find one!"

"Let's go plant hunting and see what happens," muttered Slime Fungus.

"Keep smiling!" quacked the *Dithering Duck*.

"Oh, shut up," said Whiff Erik in a choked voice.

***

All that day, Whiff Erik and Slime Fungus filled their collecting boxes with wild flowers and plants. But, just as Whiff Erik had predicted, people ran away when they saw them.

Poor Whiff Erik! He tried to apologise for the trouble caused by Spike Carbuncle and Axehead.

"Not all Vikings have such terrible manners," he would say, reaching into his pocket. "Please take these gold coins and put a really thick door on your cottage."

By the end of the day, word had spread among the islanders that the one with the lank, black hair who smelled really awful was actually a nice Viking. The problem was the other one.

And so, as Whiff Erik and Slime Fungus were returning to the *Dithering Duck*, they met a group of islanders, each carrying an armful of vegetables.

"Oh, smelly, nice Viking," cried a man in a goatskin tunic with a circle of vines around his head. "As chief of this island, please, I beg you to accept these gifts and take the bad, nasty Viking away from here."

Whiff Erik didn't know what to do. Spike Carbuncle had never done what he was told, no matter who asked, so the chances of getting him to leave the island were zero. But the islanders looked so miserable that Whiff Erik agreed to try.

"Where is he?"

The islanders turned and pointed to the beach.

Spike Carbuncle and Axehead were swigging mugs of beer and fighting over a huge pile of gold and jewellery. A few feet away, the *Stealthy Stoat* was egging them on, its greedy eyes glittering in the setting sun.

Whiff Erik looked at the chief. Now was his last chance to find a bride.

"Are there any other islands near here?" asked Whiff Erik, hopefully. Because so far he hadn't seen a pretty girl, or even an ugly one, anywhere.

The man with the vine leaves in his hair shook his head. "The closest island is three full moons away."

Whiff Erik's heart sank as he remembered his mother's command. They had to return by the next full moon with a bride. The son who brought back the bride she liked best would rule Goose Pimple Bay. The other would be banished to the forest for ever.

With a heavy heart, Whiff Erik thanked the chief and trudged down to the shore.

The only good thing was that Spike Carbuncle obviously hadn't found a bride, either. So at least that meant they were both doomed.

Ten minutes later, Whiff Erik couldn't believe his ears.

"OK," said Spike Carbuncle. "I'll go." He turned towards the *Stealthy Stoat*. "I've got everything I want from here."

Chapter Four

"Oi, you! Stinkhead!"

The *Dithering Duck* had been at sea for a morning when a voice like nails scraping a blackboard suddenly filled the air.

Whiff Erik went white, as a thing that looked more like a wolverine than a girl clambered over the side. The remains of her small, wooden boat sank in the water.

"Bat got your tongue?" asked the girl. She held her huge nose with her claw-like fingers. "Yuck! Have you rolled in something?"

Whiff Erik was so stunned by the girl's ugly face and her incredible rudeness that he could only splutter, "Of course not! Only dogs do that."

"Huh," said the girl suspiciously. "There's a first time for everything."

"Who are you?" demanded Whiff Erik. "And what are you doing on my boat?"

"The name's Fangtrude and I want a lift."

"Where to?"

"Where are you going?"

"Home," said Whiff Erik.

A grin full of pointed teeth spread over Fangtrude's dirty, stubby face "Good! Then I'm coming, too!" She pointed to a box of neatly arranged plants and vegetables. "What's that load of garbage?"

"That's my collection," replied Whiff Erik, in a hurt voice. "I'm a very keen gardener, you see."

"You mean you're a sissy that stinks," sneered Fangtrude.

Slime Fungus looked up from where he was chewing on an old root. "She won't do as a bride," he muttered. "Throw her overboard before Ma Moosejaw sees her on your boat."

Thwack! Fangtrude's foot met Slime Fungus's ear and he slumped slowly onto the wooden planks. "OK, poo face," she snarled at Whiff Erik. "What's all this stuff about brides? Tell me! Now!"

Whiff Erik stared at the girl's glittering, red eyes and her spiky, black hair. He knew that strange things often happened. The *Dithering Duck* was always telling him that kind of stuff. But he never really believed it.

Surely this disgusting girl wasn't meant to be his bride? What about the pretty girl with the blonde hair from his dreams?

Whiff Erik believed in dreams. He had done ever since he was a child.

"Dreams don't come true," quacked the *Dithering Duck*, reading his master's mind. "Especially ones about brides with blonde hair and blue eyes."

"What's that dumb duck talking about?" demanded Fangtrude. Her eyes narrowed. "Are you by any chance looking for a bride?"

Whiff Erik felt his stomach turn over. Even if it meant losing the kingdom to his brother, he couldn't marry this girl. He would rather hoe carrots for the rest of his life, alone in the forest. "Absolutely not," he said firmly. "I will never marry anyone, ever."

✳✳✳

"Hey, Spike," called Axehead from below deck on the *Stealthy Stoat*. "There's a sack wriggling in here."

"Of course it's wriggling," muttered Spike Carbuncle. "It's full of goats."

"Not that one. This one." As he spoke, Axehead heaved a sack onto the deck and untied it. A pretty girl with blonde hair stepped out.

"Which one of you is Spike?" she asked, sweetly. "I heard you both talking."

"What's it to you?" Spike Carbuncle stared at the girl. She was the kind that really made him feel sick. It was the blonde hair, the blue eyes and the sweet voice. Besides, any girl that hadn't tried to kick him after he'd tied her up in  a sack with only a few biscuits to eat must be a real weedy wet. Why on earth hadn't he looked at her before he'd stuffed her below deck?

"Because it was night," hissed the *Stealthy Stoat*, reading Spike Carbuncle's mind. "How many times have I told you to take a candle when it's dark?"

The girl looked at Spike's mean, greasy face. "If you don't mind my saying, you look as if you should be eating more vegetables," she said in a voice that reminded Spike of his mother. She pulled out a carrot from her pocket. "My name is Fernsilver and I believe in eating healthy food."

Axehead looked up from where he was chewing on a piece of salted reindeer hide. "She'll be no good as a bride," he muttered. "Throw her overboard before Ma Moosejaw sees her on your boat."

But Fernsilver was peering into Spike Carbuncle's face. "When was the last time you ate raw spinach?" she asked, reaching into her other pocket.

"No, no!" Spike held out his hands to push the awful girl away. The truth was, he was terrified of spinach. Lately he'd been having nightmares about spinach leaves falling on his face like huge, green snowflakes and suffocating him.

"Don't be silly, Spike," said Fernsilver. "Vegetables are good for you." She smiled at his grey face. "Now, what's all this talk about brides? Is that why you asked me to come home with you?"

"I didn't ask you anything," muttered Spike Carbuncle, who couldn't bring himself to meet Fernsilver's big, blue eyes. "I stuffed you in a sack and it was a big mistake."

"No, it wasn't," replied Fernsilver gently. She moved closer to him. "Don't be shy. You see, I can help you." She paused and said in a more determined voice. "Also, when you stuffed me in a sack, you took my goats, and I will never be parted from them. So now you've got them, you've got me."

Spike Carbuncle felt his stomach turn over. He was sure his mother and father would think he had chosen this girl as his bride as soon they saw her on his boat. But even if it meant losing the kingdom to his brother, Spike Carbuncle knew he couldn't marry Fernsilver. She would drive him nuts. Besides, he hated goats. He would rather be banished to the forest and live off burnt bear meat.

"I do not want to marry you," shouted Spike Carbuncle. "I will never marry anyone, ever!"

The sun was setting as the *Stealthy Stoat* and the *Dithering Duck* pulled into Goose Pimple Bay. And it wasn't a day too soon for Whiff Erik. One more night with Fangtrude and, even though he knew it was wrong, he was sure he would have thrown her overboard. He had never met such a bad-tempered, foul-mouthed, nasty girl in his whole life.

She was just like Spike Carbuncle!

As for Spike Carbuncle, the thought of another day listening to Fernsilver talking about her goats, or how vegetables were so good for you made his fingers itch to stuff her back in a sack and knot it really tightly.

She was just like Whiff Erik!

As the boats landed, Ma Moosejaw and Chief Thunderstruck waited on the wooden quay. Behind them, the men and women of Goose Pimple Bay waited, too.

"STOP!" bellowed Ma Moosejaw. She held up her hand as Spike Carbuncle and Whiff Erik began to unload their cargo. "We don't want to see that stuff. Where are your brides?"

Spike Carbuncle and Whiff Erik exchanged looks. For the first time ever they had something in common. And that was TERROR! What if their mother made them marry the girls on their boats?

Chapter Five

"**W**here are your brides?" shouted Ma Moosejaw again. "You must marry them at once!" She stomped her great foot on the ground. "Then I will choose the son who will rule the kingdom! And the other will be banished to the forest for ever!"

Both Spike Carbuncle and Whiff Erik thought they were going to be sick.

What were they going to do?

Then Fangtrude appeared from the hold of the *Dithering Duck* and Fernsilver walked across the deck of the *Stealthy Stoat*.

Both brothers stared in amazement.

The pretty blonde girl was the one in Whiff Erik's dreams!

Spike Carbuncle looked into Fangtrude's glittering, red eyes and felt himself falling into an abyss of love!

"Who is that girl?" Whiff Erik asked Spike Carbuncle.

"Fernsilver," muttered Spike Carbuncle out of the corner of his mouth. "I found her on the island. She's awful. All she talks about is goats and vegetables."

"Step forward with your brides!" yelled Ma Moosejaw. She signalled to a man in a long, white robe. "Marry them both, *now*!"

"But Ma!" wailed Spike Carbuncle and Whiff Erik at the same time. "You don't understand! There's been a—"

"A what?" interrupted Ma Moosejaw. She narrowed her eyes. "There's been a *what*?"

Whiff Erik and Spike Carbuncle knew that trying to explain anything even slightly complicated to their mother was impossible.

Desperate measures were called for!

Spike Carbuncle leapt onto the *Dithering Duck* and bent down on one knee in front of Fangtrude. "Will you marry me?" he asked in a trembling voice.

Fangtrude whacked him across the face. "Sure," she snarled. "But I give the orders, OK?"

"OK," whispered Spike Carbuncle, happily, and he led Fangtrude onto the quay and up to the man in the long, white robe.

Quick as flash, Whiff Erik jumped into the *Stealthy Stoat* and knelt down in front of Fernsilver. "Will you accept my hand in marriage and my vegetables for ever?" he asked.

"Can I bring my goats?" said Fernsilver.
Whiff Erik nodded. "Of course!"

"Then I will," said Fernsilver. "Because now I know it was my fate to come here." She smiled. "I've met you in my dreams."

Fernsilver and Erik followed Spike and Fangtrude along the quay.

"Get on with it!" cried Ma Moosejaw to the man in the long, white robe. Then she turned to the men and women of Goose Pimple Bay. "You are all invited to the wedding supper. I will announce my decision in the morning!"

✳✳✳

That night, Ma Moosejaw tossed and turned in her bed. The memory of the wedding supper wouldn't go away. It had been terrible. Fangtrude had thrown her food on the floor and refused to share the fire-breathing lizard. Everything about her was mean, nasty and rude.

On the other hand, everyone had taken a liking to Fernsilver. Especially since she had talked Whiff Erik into having a bath and introduced them to a new food called batter pudding, which she made with lots of flour and milk and eggs all mixed up together and cooked in the great bread oven. It tasted delicious. Especially with roast beef. In fact, everything about Fernsilver was kind, thoughtful and sensible.

Ma Moosejaw woke up with a heavy heart. "What am I going to do?" she asked Chief Thunderstruck.

"Follow your gut instinct," he replied. "It's the only way."

Ma Moosejaw looked at her stomach and thought hard. It didn't seem to help.

"I mean do what you feel is the right thing," said Chief Thunderstruck, patiently. "Choose the bride you like best."

"I hate Fangtrude," said Ma Moosejaw firmly.

"Then there's your answer!" cried Chief Thunderstruck. He jumped out of bed. "Now, let's make the announcement and get out of here! I've booked our sledge for after breakfast."

The Great Hall was silent as the last of the lumpy porridge was cleared away. All along each side of the long table, everyone was looking very, very nervous.

At last, Ma Moosejaw stood up. "I have come to a decision," she said in an important voice. "And—"

But before she could finish, Fangtrude jumped up onto her stool. "So have I," she yelled. "So shut up and listen!" She fixed Ma Moosejaw with her glittering, red eyes. "No one is banishing anyone to the forest, Mooseface, because there isn't going to be any choice!"

"*What?*" A gasp went around the room.

"I said, shut up and listen," shouted Fangtrude, again. "On my island, it's the girls who go off to find a husband." She grabbed Spike Carbuncle by the hair, slammed his head on the table and put her foot on his neck. "So you're coming with me. Got it?"

"Got it," whispered Spike Carbuncle in a dreamy voice.

"Good!" yelled Fangtrude. "Then pack your sack! We're out of here!"

"See you later, sucker," said Spike Carbuncle to Whiff Erik as Fangtrude dragged him out of the door

"Good luck, son!" cried Chief Thunderstruck.

"He'll need it where he's going," cackled Fangtrude. Then she stuck out her tongue at Ma Moosejaw and slammed the door behind her.

For a second there was complete silence. Then Ma Moosejaw led Whiff Erik and Fernsilver to the top of the table and all the men and women and children in the Great Hall of Goose Pimple Bay began to clap and cheer and stamp their feet with joy.

***

An hour later, Ma Moosejaw climbed onto the back of the brand-new sledge that was to take her all the way north to the land of the ice palaces and white bears. She was wearing her special beaver-skin cloak and her wolf-tail hat.

Ma Moosejaw had never been so happy. "The best bit of my life begins now!" she hooted, waving her hands in the air.

In front of her, Chief Thunderstruck stepped into the driver's seat and picked up the reins. Ten huge dogs began to bark furiously and jump up and down.

"Bye, bye, darlings," shouted Ma Moosejaw to Whiff Erik and Fernsilver, as they stood in front of the door to the Great Hall. "We'll send you a—" but no one ever found out what that was going to be because at that moment Chief Thunderstruck cracked his whip and they set off.

Whiff Erik stared at the sledge that was taking his mother far, far away for a very, very long time. Then he stared at Fernsilver and felt his heart soar in his chest.

The *Dithering Duck* was wrong.

Sometimes dreams *do* come true!

THE GOOSE PIMPLE BAY · SAGAS ·

Whiff Erik
and the
Great Green Thing

"It had sharp, green teeth and a face like a lumpy, green root."

Whiff Erik is crazy about vegetables!
So when he discovers his brother, Spike,
has a rare seed, he just has to have it.
He plants it in Goose Pimple Bay. But it's not
long before a gigantic plant blots out the
sky and a great green thing appears in
the leaves. Oh dear, Whiff Erik knows
they're in big, big, trouble . . .

**The second hilarious adventure in
The Goose Pimple Bay Sagas**

Available Now!